PUFFIN BOOKS

Why does my mum ALWAYS iron a crease in my Jeans?

Fiona Waters is one of the most prolific and, quite simply, best anthologists in the children's book world. Her work includes *Glitter When You Jump*, *The Poetry Book*, *Love* and *Don't Panic: 100 Poems to Save Your Life*. Her unparalleled knowledge of poetry and children's books has come about, in part, through Fiona's previous incarnations as a bookseller, publisher, reviewer, author and current position as Editorial Director of Troubadour, the highly successful school book fair company.

Fiona lives in Dorset among thousands of books and some very discerning cats.

"Why does my mum always iron a crease in my jeans?"

PUFFIN

PUFFIN BOOKS

Penguin Books Ltd, 80 Strand, London WC2R 0RL, England
Penguin Group (USA) Inc., 375 Hudson Street, New York, New York 10014, USA
Penguin Group (Canada), 10 Alcorn Avenue, Toronto, Ontario, Canada M4V 3B2
(a division of Pearson Penguin Canada Inc.)
Penguin Ireland, 25 St Stephen's Green, Dublin 2, Ireland (a division of Penguin Books Ltd)
Penguin Group (Australia), 250 Camberwell Road, Camberwell, Victoria 3124, Australia
(a division of Pearson Australia Group Pty Ltd)
Penguin Books India Pvt Ltd, 11 Community Centre, Panchsheel Park, New Delhi – 110 017, India
Penguin Group (NZ), cnr Airborne and Rosedale Roads, Albany, Auckland 1310, New Zealand
(a division of Pearson New Zealand Ltd)
Penguin Books (South Africa) (Pty) Ltd, 24 Sturdee Avenue, Rosebank 2196, South Africa

Penguin Books Ltd, Registered Offices: 80 Strand, London WC2R 0RL, England

www.penguin.com

First published 2005
I

The Acknowledgements on pages 137–144 constitute an
extension of this copyright page

Typeset in Bembo by Palimpsest Book Production Limited
Polmont, Stirlingshire

Made and printed in England by Clays Ltd, St Ives plc

British Library Cataloguing in Publication Data
A CIP catalogue record for this book is available from the British Library

ISBN 0–141–31529–6

Remembering Linda, with much love

contents

EXCITEMENT IS NOT WHAT I COME TO
  SCHOOL FOR
Why? *Lindsay MacRae*   3
Stale *Ian McMillan*   5
January 7 *Stephen Knight*   6
Seen Through *Alan Durant*   7
Kelly Jane Dancing *Fred Sedgwick*   8
The King and the Wind *John Rice*   9
What the Wind Said *Russell Hoban*   10
What Are You More Afraid Of? *Stephen Knight*   11
Don't Be Scared *Carol Ann Duffy*   12
Poem for the Changing of the Clocks *Gerard Benson*   13
It's Only the Storm *David Greygoose*   15
Storm *Gillian Clarke*   16
Late July *Stephen Knight*   17
For a Junior School Poetry Book *Christopher Middleton*   18
Miss Creedle Teaches Creative Writing *Gareth Owen*   19
Colour of My Dreams *Peter Dixon*   23

THE FOOTPRINTS ARE NEVER MINE
Listen Mr Oxford don *John Agard*   27
Indian Children Speak *Juanita Bell*   29
What's Your Colour? *Julia Donaldson*   31
Okay, Brown Girl, Okay *James Berry*   33
Perfect Paula *Lindsay MacRae*   35
About Friends *Brian Jones*   36
Haiku *Mike Jubb*   38
Piggy to Joey *Stevie Smith*   39

The Side Way Back   *Philip Gross*   40
The Bully   *Adrian Mitchell*   42
Billy's Coming Back   *Brian Moses*   43
Lucky   *Roger McGough*   45
Letting Her Go   *Alan Durant*   48
For Golden Ella   *Adrian Mitchell*   50
Hens   *Evelyn Conlon*   51
Strangeways   *Roger McGough*   54
What Have We Got in the House?   *Nick Toczek*   55
Unicorn   *John Cotton*   57
In a dark stone   *Jenny Joseph*   58
A Feather From an Angel   *Brian Moses*   61
The Fairy Sea   *Patricia P. Jones*   63
A Bargain   *Richard Edwards*   65
Mirrors   *Isobel Thrilling*   66
From *Fairy Tales*   *Lee Cataldi*   67
A Place Without Footprints   *Daphne Kitching*   68
Image   *T. E. Hulme*   70
Suit of Armor   *Beverly McLoughland*   71
Shell   *Ted Hughes*   72

ARE WE GOING SEPARATE WAYS?
Happiness   *Raymond Carver*   75
One-track Mind   *Sophie Hannah*   76
Mir Baku   *Lucy Coats*   77
Middle Child   *Lindsay MacRae*   78
Dad's Night Voice   *James Berry*   79
Dad, Don't Dance   *Roger Stevens*   80
Divorce: A Spell to Prevent It   *Lindsay MacRae*   82
Granny   *Pam Zinnemann-Hope*   84
Kelly Jane Alone   *Fred Sedgwick*   86
On the Elevator Going Down   *Richard Brautigan*   88
Answer Phone   *John Mole*   90

NOW I'M TOO COMPLICATED

Love Without Hope   *Robert Graves*   93
Leonardo   *Charles Causley*   94
Fearless Bushmen   *Benjamin Zephaniah*   96
Kaleidoscope   *Michael Rosen*   98
Just For Fun   *Richard Edwards*   103
Growing Apples   *Michael Rosen*   105
The Tunneller   *Wes Magee*   108
Dead End   *Michael Harrison*   110
I Was Afraid to Begin   *Seamus Cashman*   111
A Sort of Chinese Poem   *Elizabeth Jennings*   112
Spellbound   *Norman Vandal*   113
Shop Chat   *Libby Houston*   114
Against Broccoli   *Roy Blount, Jr*   115
Lizzie's Road   *Gervase Phinn*   116
Everything in its Place   *Arthur Guiterman*   117
I'll Bark Against the Dog-star   *Anonymous*   118
Spell to Summon the Owner of the Shoes   *Jeni Couzyn*   119
How to Talk to Trees   *Gillian Floyd*   121
Whosland   *Benjamin Zephaniah*   123
Child-body Starving Story   *James Berry*   125
The Sun and the Lizard   *Zulfikar Ghose*   127
First Morning   *John Agard*   128
Thoughts Like an Ocean   *Gareth Owen*   129
Steam in the Kettle   *Charles Causley*   131
On Visiting a Natural History Museum   *Isobel Thrilling*   134

Acknowledgements   137
Index of First Lines   145
Index of Poets   149

EXCITEMENT IS NOT WHAT I COME TO SCHOOL FOR

Why?

Why is just a minute
always several hours?

Why does 'I'll think about it'
always mean you won't?

Why are books good for you
and comics bad,
when they've both got words in them?

Why, if oranges are called oranges
because they're orange,
aren't bananas called yellows?

Why don't they supply batteries
when they sell you a hamster
so that it will have enough energy
to whiz round on its exercise wheel
when your friends visit?

Why does my sister
always cover her spots
with something more noticeable
than the spot is?

Why does my mum always
iron a crease in my jeans?

Why do people always say
'It really suits you'
when you've just had the world's
worst haircut?

And why, if we can go to the moon,
don't we go there more often?

LINDSAY MACRAE

stale

You know how sometimes
you open your sandwich box
and it smells stale

and there are a few crumbs
and a biscuit wrapper
and a bit of a crisp

and you want to close it
although you know you should wash it
you want to close it.

Well, that's how I feel today.

IAN MCMILLAN

January 7

My father left us in the dead of winter.
Snow shut the door. Snow turned the key.
My father left us in the dead of winter.
Now I leave blank the pages of my diary.

STEPHEN KNIGHT

seen Through

'You look good in glasses.
    You know, sort of pretty,
brainy too,' I said.
'They suit your face,
the shape of your head.'
'Yeah, well, you can get
stuffed an' all,' she said.

ALAN DURANT

Kelly Jane Dancing

When I'm dancing
when I'm dancing
my hair flies around
and I feel the rhythm thumping
to my feet on the ground.
I feel my heart speeding
and my eyes flashing clear –
my body's alive
when I'm dancing.

FRED SEDGWICK

The King and the Wind

'Come,' said the King,
   'come and all these I shall give to you:

   a moated castle with knights to protect you,
   a banqueting hall with servants to feed you,
   a treasure chest with silver to please you.'

'Stay,' said the Wind,
'stay and all these shall I give to you:

   a sky with clouds ever changing,
   a mountain with glens ever singing,
   a shore with waves ever dancing.'

'Come,' said the King; 'Stay,' said the Wind.

JOHN RICE

What the Wind said

'Far away is where I've come from,' said
the wind.
'Guess what I've brought you.'
        'What?' I asked.
'Shadows dancing on a brown road by an old
Stone fence,' the wind said. 'Do you like that?'
        'Yes,' I said. 'What else?'
'Daisies nodding, and the drone of one small
  airplane
In a sleepy sky,' the wind continued.
        'I like the airplane, and the daisies too,' I
        said.
        'What else!'
'That's not enough?' the wind complained.
        'No,' I said. 'I want the song that you
        were singing.
        Give me that.'
'That's mine,' the wind said. 'Find your own.'
        And left.

RUSSELL HOBAN

What Are you more Afraid Of?

A noise in the house
or no noise at all?
The instant before
or after the fall?

Fire or water?
In woods after dark
or alone in a boat?
A bear or a shark?

A river to cross
or a mountain to climb?
Saying goodbye with
too much or no time?

The breeze of your breath?
The knock of your heart?
Creatures that slither
or creatures that dart?

STEPHEN KNIGHT

Don't Be Scared

The dark is only a blanket
for the moon to put on her bed.

The dark is a private cinema
for the movie dreams in your head.

The dark is a little black dress
to show off the sequin stars.

The dark is the wooden hole
behind the strings of happy guitars.

The dark is a jeweller's velvet cloth
where children sleep like pearls.

The dark is a spool of film
to photograph boys and girls,

so smile in your sleep in the dark.
Don't be scared.

CAROL ANN DUFFY

poem for the changing of the clocks

This hour
  in the night
    When I wait
     in the dark
      bedroom
        for sleep to take me away
Passes with tick
  and tock
   of the wooden clock,
And I hear also
  in my imagination
    The silent breathing
     in   out
      in   out
Of a thousand other
  listeners to the night.
Cats stalk the slates
On firm and soundless feet
And tear the darkness with their yowls.
The joists and timbers
  stretch and sigh,

Ghosts in the attic creak.
   And dew beads the listening sycamore
That inks the space
   between me and the indifferent moon.

And this is the hour, perhaps
That will never be,
That will be looped into time
As the clocks of England
Adjust after their long summer
   To the rigours of Greenwich.

A child turns in its sleep
and somewhere an aged tap
   drips
           and
                   drips.

GERARD BENSON

It's Only the Storm

'What's that creature that rattles the roof?'
'Hush, it's only the storm.'

'What's blowing the tiles and the branches off?'
'Hush, it's only the storm.'

'What's riding the sky like a wild white horse,
Flashing its teeth and stamping its hooves?'

'Hush, my dear, it's only the storm,
Racing the darkness till it catches the dawn.
Hush, my dear, it's only the storm,
When you wake in the morning, it will be gone.'

DAVID GREYGOOSE

Storm

The cat lies low, too scared
to cross the garden.

For two days we are bowed
by a whiplash of hurricane.

The hill's a wind-harp.
Our bones are flutes of ice.

The heart drums in its small room
and the river rattles its pebbles.

Thistlefields are comb and paper
whisperings of syllable and bone

till no word's left
but thud and rumble of

something with hooves or wheels,
something breathing too hard.

GILLIAN CLARKE

Late July

What happens when the gates are locked
and summer starts, beyond the playground's
chain-link fence, that famous puddle
dry in the centre circle, and blades of grass
back in the goalmouths worn to mud
all term, a solitary sick-note
fading on a staffroom window sill,
the registers completed for another year?

The long days hang from us like stones.
They drag us to the earth. They make us sleep.
And while we sleep, our voices break,
our faces change, our clothes tear at the seams.
We are lost in fields, in woods, in towns.
We will never be the same again.

STEPHEN KNIGHT

For a Junior School Poetry Book

The mothers are waiting in the yard.
Here come the children, fresh from school.
The mothers are wearing rumpled skirts.
What prim mouths, what wrinkly cheeks.
The children swirl through the air to them,
trailing satchels and a smell of chalk.

The children are waiting in the yard.
The mothers come stumbling out of school.
The children stare primly at them,
lace their shoes, pat their heads.
The mothers swirl through the air to cars.
The children crossly drive them home.

The mothers are coming.
The children are waiting.
The mothers had eyes that see
boiled eggs, wool, dung and bed.
The children have eyes that saw
owl and mountain and little mole.

CHRISTOPHER MIDDLETON

Miss Creedle Teaches creative writing

'This morning,' cries Miss Creedle,
    'We're all going to use our imaginations,
We're going to close our eyes 3W and imagine.
Are we ready to imagine Darren?
I'm going to count to three.
At one, we wipe our brains completely clean;
At two, we close our eyes;
And at three, we imagine.
Are we all imagining? Good.
Here is a piece of music by Beethoven to help
    us.
Beethoven's dates were 1770 to 1827.
(See The Age of Revolutions in your History
    books.)
Although Beethoven was deaf and a German
He wrote many wonderful symphonies,
But this was a long time before anyone of us
    was born.
Are you imagining a time before you were born?
What does it look like? Is it dark?
(Embryo is a good word you might use.)
Does the music carry you away like a river?
What is the name of the river? Can you smell
    it?

Foetid is an exciting adjective.
As you float down the river
Perhaps you land on an alien planet.
Tell me what sounds you hear.
If there are indescribable monsters
Tell me what they look like but not now.
(Your book entitled *Tackle Pre-History This Way*
Will be of assistance here.)
Perhaps you are cast adrift in a broken barrel.
In stormy shark-infested waters
(Remember the work we did on piranhas for
  R.E.?)
Try to see yourself. Can you do that?
See yourself at the bottom of a pothole in the
  Andes
With both legs broken
And your life ebbing away inexorably.
What does the limestone feel like?
See the colours.
Have you done that? Good.
And now you may open your eyes.
Your imagining time is over,
Now it is writing time.
Are we ready to write? Good.
Then write away.
Wayne, you're getting some exciting ideas down.
Tracy, that's lovely.
Darren, you haven't written anything.

Couldn't you put the date?
You can't think of anything to write.
Well, what did you see when you closed your
   eyes?
But you must have seen something beside the
   black.
Yes, apart from the little squiggles.
Just the black. I see.
Well, try to think
Of as many words as you can.'

Miss Creedle whirls about the class
Like a benign typhoon
Spinning from one quailing homestead to
   another.
I dream of peaceful ancient days
In Mr Swindell's class
When the hours passed like a dream
Filled with order and measuring and tests.
Excitement is not one of the things I come to
   school for.
I force my eyes shut
Kicking ineffectually at the starter;
But all I see
Is a boy of twelve
Sitting at a desk one dark November day
Writing this poem.
And Darren is happy to discover

There is only one word for black
And that will have to suffice
Until the bell rings for all of us.

GARETH OWEN

colour of my Dreams

I'm a really rotten reader
the worst in all the class,
the sort of rotten reader
that makes you want to laugh.

I'm last in all the readin' tests,
my score's not on the page
and when I read to teacher
she gets in such a rage.

She says I cannot form my words
she says I can't build up
and that I don't know phonics
– and don't know c-a-t from k-u-p.

They say that I'm dyxlectic
(that's a word they've just found out)
. . . but when I get some plasticine
I know what that's about.

I make these scary monsters
I draw these secret lands
and get my hair all sticky
and paint on all me hands.

I make these super models,

I build these smashing towers
that reach up to the ceiling
– and take me hours and hours.

I paint these lovely pictures
in thick green drippy paint
that gets all on the carpet –
and makes the cleaners faint.

I build great magic forests
weave bushes out of string
and paint pink panderellos
and birds that really sing.

I play my world of real believe
I play it every day
and teachers stand and watch me
but don't know what to say.

They give me diagnostic tests,
they try out reading schemes,
but none of them will ever know
the colour of my dreams.

PETER DIXON

THE FOOTPRINTS ARE NEVER MINE

Listen mr Oxford don

Me not no Oxford don
me a simple immigrant
from Clapham Common
I didn't graduate
I immigrate

But listen Mr Oxford don
I'm a man on de run
and a man on de run
is a dangerous one

I ent have no gun
I ent have no knife
but mugging de Queen's English
is the story of my life

I dont need no axe
to split/ up yu syntax
I dont need no hammer
to mash/ up yu grammar

I warning you Mr Oxford don
I'm a wanted man
and a wanted man
is a dangerous one

Dem accuse me of assault
on de Oxford dictionary/
imagine a concise peaceful man like me/
dem want me serve time
for inciting rhyme to riot
but I tekking it quiet
down here in Clapham Common

I'm not a violent man Mr Oxford don
I only armed wit mih human breath
but human breath
is a dangerous weapon

So mek dem send one big word after me
I ent serving no jail sentence
I slashing suffix in self-defence
I bashing future wit present tense
and if necessary

I making de Queen's English accessory/to my
    offence

JOHN AGARD

Indian children speak

People said, 'Indian children are hard to
teach.
Don't expect them to talk.'
One day stubby little Boy said,
'Last night the moon went all the way with
me,
When I went out to walk.'
People said, 'Indian children are very silent.
Their only words are no and yes.'
But, ragged Pansy confided softly,
'My dress is old, but at night the moon is kind;
Then I wear a beautiful moon-colored dress.'
People said, 'Indian children are dumb.
They seldom make a reply.'
Clearly I hear Delores answer,
'Yes, the sunset is so good, I think God is throwing
A bright shawl around the shoulders of the
sky.'
People said, 'Indian children have no affection.
They just don't care for anyone.'
Then I feel Ramon's hand and hear him whisper,
'A wild animal races in me since my mother
sleeps
under the ground. Will it always run and run?'
People said, 'Indian children are rude.
They don't seem very bright.'

Then I remember Joe Henry's remark,
'The tree is hanging down her head because
  the sun
is staring at her. White people always stare.
They do not know it is not polite.'
People said, 'Indian children never take you in,
Outside their thoughts you'll always stand.'
I have forgotten the idle words that People said,
But treasure the day when iron doors swung
  wide,
And I slipped into the heart of Indian Land.

JUANITA BELL

What's your colour?

What's your colour, the colour of your skin,
The colour of the envelope that you're
wrapped in?

Is it like chocolate, tea or coffee?
Is it like marzipan, fudge or toffee?
Peaches and cream or a strawberry milk shake
Or does it look more like a curranty cake?

What's your colour, the colour of your skin,
The colour of the envelope that you're wrapped
in?

Are you a map of your past disasters?
Grazes and scratches and sticking plasters?
Bites from mosquitoes, a yellow–blue bruise
And a couple of blisters from rather tight shoes?

What's your colour, the colour of your skin,
The colour of the envelope that you're wrapped
in?

How does it go when the weather's sunny?
Brown as a berry or gold as honey?
Does it go freckly or peeling and sore?
Is there a mark from the watch that you wore?

What's your colour, the colour of your skin,
The colour of the envelope that you're
  wrapped in?

Do you go pink when you're all embarrassed?
Sweaty and red when you're hot and harassed?
Bumpy and blue on a cold winter's day?
When it's time for your bath are you usually
  grey?

What's your colour, the colour of your skin,
The colour of the envelope that you're wrapped
  in?

JULIA DONALDSON

Okay, Brown Girl, Okay

for Josie, nine years old, who wrote to me saying,
'Boys called me names because of my colour. I felt
very upset . . . my brother and sister are English. I
wish I was, then I won't be picked on . . . How do
you like being brown?'

Josie, Josie, I am okay
being brown. I remember,
every day dusk and dawn get born
from the loving of night and light
who work together, like married.
> And they would like to say to you:
> Be at school on and on, brown Josie
> like thousands and thousands and
> > thousands
> of children, who are brown and white
> and black and pale-lemon colour.
> All the time, brown girl Josie is okay.

Josie, Josie, I am okay
being brown. I remember,
every minute sun in the sky
and ground of the earth work together
like married.
> And they would like to say to you:
> Ride on up a going escalator

like thousands and thousands and
  thousands
of people, who are brown and white
and black and pale-lemon colour.
All the time, brown girl Josie is okay.

Josie, Josie, I am okay
being brown. I remember,
all the time bright-sky and brown-earth
work together, like married
making forests and food and flowers and rain.
    And they would like to say to you:
    Grow and grow brightly, brown girl.
    Write and read and play and work.
    Ride bus or train or boat or aeroplane
    like thousands and thousands and
      thousands
    of children, who are brown and white
    and black and pale-lemon colour.
    All the time, brown girl Josie is okay.

JAMES BERRY

34

perfect paula

Paula is tidy
  Paula is good
Paula does everything
nice girls should.

All of the teachers
think Paula is sweet.
But all of our class
know that Paula's a creep.

LINDSAY MACRAE

he good thing about friends
is not having to finish sentences.

I sat a whole summer afternoon with my friend
  once
on a river bank, bashing heels on the baked
  mud
and watching the small chunks slide into the
  water
and listening to them – plop plop plop.
He said 'I like the twigs when they . . . you
  know . . .
like that.' I said 'There's that branch . . .'
We both said 'Mmmm.' The river flowed and
  flowed
and there were lots of butterflies, that afternoon.

I first thought there was a sad thing about friends
when we met twenty years later.
We both talked hundreds of sentences,
taking care to finish all we said,
and explain it all very carefully,
as if we'd been discovered in places
we should not be, and were somehow ashamed.

I understood then what the river meant by flowing.

BRIAN JONES

Haiku

I was daydreaming
about being popular,
and it made me smile.

MIKE JUBB

Piggy to Joey

Piggy to Joey,
  Piggy to Joe,
Yes, that's what I was –
Piggy to Joe.

Will he come back again?
Oh no, no, no.
Oh how I wish I hadn't been
Piggy to Joe.

Stevie Smith

The side way Back

You're late. Take a chance up the cul-de-sac,
a short cut home. It's the side way back –
the way they tell you not to go,
the way the kids and stray cats know
as Lovebite Alley, Dead Dog Lane . . .
The Council says it's got no name.

All the same . . .

There's sharkstooth glass on a breezeblock wall.
There's nobody near to hear if you call.
There are tetanus tips on the rusty wire.
There's a house they bricked up after the fire
spraycanned with blunt names and a thinks-
   balloon
full of four-letter words and a grinning moon-
                                    cartoon.

It's a narrow and narrowing one way street
down to the end where the night kids meet.
You've seen the scuffed-out tips of their fags.
You've smelt something wrong in their
   polythene bags.
There's a snuffle and a scratching at a
   planked-up gate.

There's a footstep you don't hear till almost
 too late.

                              Don't wait.

Now you're off and you're running for years
 and years
with the hissing of panic like rain in your ears.
You could run till you're old, you could run
 till you're gone
and never get home. To slow down and walk on
is hard. Harder still is to turn
and look back. Though it's slow as a Chinese burn,
                              you'll learn.

PHILIP GROSS

The Bully

His head was a helmet
His muscles sprung steel
Each finger was
An electric eel
He was merciless
As the Bloody Tower
I was eight years old
And I was in his power

ADRIAN MITCHELL

Billy's coming back

W ord is out on the street tonight,
Billy's coming back.

There's a sound outside of running feet,
somebody, somewhere's switched on the heat,
policemen are beating a swift retreat
now Billy's coming back.

Only last year when he went away
everyone heaved a sigh,
now news is out, and the neighbourhood
is set to blow sky-high.

Words are heard in the staffroom,
teachers' faces deepen with gloom,
can't shrug off this feeling of doom
now Billy's coming back.

It was wonderful when he upped and left,
a carnival feeling straightaway,
no looking over shoulders,
each day was a holiday.

And now like a bomb no one dares defuse,
time ticks on while kids quake in their shoes.

No winners here, you can only lose,
now Billy's coming back.

It's dog eat dog on the street tonight,
it's cat and mouse, Billy's looking for a fight,
so take my advice, keep well out of sight
now Billy's coming back.

BRIAN MOSES

Lucky

There was a boy at school we called 'Lucky'
  All he did was whinge and moan
'Lucky' was the nickname we gave him
  Because he was so accident-prone

If something was spilled or knocked over
  Splattered, burnt or bust
There in the midst of the damage
  Would be Lucky looking nonplussed

He said that bad things happened to him
  Having been born under an unlucky star
And a fortune-teller warned his mother
  Not to let him travel far

So to ward off every kind of harm
  The gypsy gave him a lucky charm:
A silver horseshoe, rabbit's paw,
  Lucky heather, eagle's claw,
Coloured glass and polished stones
  Dried hair and yellowing bones

He never walked under ladders
  Never stepped on pavement cracks
Never touched a looking-glass
  Never learned how to relax

You could spot Lucky a mile off
  Count the creases in his frown
As he concentrated on keeping alive
  His pockets weighted down

With a silver horseshoe, rabbit's paw,
  Lucky heather, eagle's claw,
Coloured glass and polished stones
  Dried hair and yellowing bones

Though the streets were full of happy kids
  He was never allowed out to play
In case of bombs, or tigers, or ghosts
  So he stayed in, out of harm's way

Then one afternoon his luck changed
  (Friday the Thirteenth, coincidentally)
He'd been kept in detention after school
  For setting fire to it (accidentally)

When hurrying home and touching wood
  For it was then well after dark
Three lads jumped him, mugged him
  Took all he had, near the gates of the park

A silver horseshoe, rabbit's paw,
  Lucky heather, eagle's claw,
Coloured glass and polished stones
  Dried hair and yellowing bones

Lucky laid low and cowered for days
  As if some tragedy would befall
But nothing unusual happened
  Nothing. Simply nothing at all

It was as if he'd been living underwater
  And at last had come up for air
Then the following week his dad won the pools
  And became a millionaire

We never saw Lucky after that
  The family moved out to Australia
So the moral is: Chuck them away
  Or doomed you'll be to failure

A silver horseshoe, rabbit's paw,
  Lucky heather, eagle's claw,
Coloured glass and polished stones
  Dried hair and yellowing bones

ROGER McGOUGH

Letting Her Go

She'd always had a baggy skin
    but now it was a bag with nothing in.
She was deaf, her fur was grey, she'd flop
    wherever.
Several times our neighbours brought her home.
Once I rescued her from the road.
'We'd better take her to the vet's,' said Dad.
I put her in the basket.
Usually she was wild and scratchy,
but tonight she went in like a mouse.
She was light as a mouse too.
Dad's voice was heavy when we sat in the car,
Puddy on my lap, soundless,
the car engine growling,
'I don't think she'll be coming back.'
I nodded, but I hadn't given up.
The vet had saved her before, maybe she would
    again.
A young cat clinked behind the counter as we
    waited.
A woman came out of the surgery with two
Siamese cats in a basket.
I smiled. They looked so bright and healthy.
Now it was our turn.
'How is she?' asked the vet and Dad shook his
    head.

The vet felt Puddy's tummy, smelt her breath,
Lifted her in the air. Puddy did nothing.
Last time she'd drawn blood.
'You know what I'm going to say,' said the vet.
'I think we should let her go, now.
I think we should do that for her.'
And then I knew.
She asked me if I wanted to stay and I did.
I stroked Puddy and whispered goodbye.
When the needle went in, Puddy crumpled
as if all her air had gone and she slipped away.
Dad bent down and kissed her head.
I kissed her too. Her fur was soft and sort of
    greasy
like it always was. Then we left,
me holding Puddy's collar, Dad with the empty
    basket.
It was raining. Dad turned on the engine
but he didn't drive away. He took my hand and
we sat staring out at the windscreen, saying
    nothing,
watching the wipers wipe away the rain,
watching the rain.

ALAN DURANT

For Golden Ella

At four in the morning
With furry tread
My good dog climbs
Aboard my bed

She lays her chin
In my open palm,
Now neither of us
Can come to harm

In my open hand
Her long jaw seems
Like a shifting weight
As she chews at her dreams

From the coolness
Of her nose
The blessing of
Her breathing glows

And the bad night
Vampires disappear
As my wrist is tickled
By her ear

ADRIAN MITCHELL

HENS

I'm a hen
Yes I'm a hen
Indeed I'm a hen
But there's one thing I'm not
And that's a bird.

You just watch me sometime
when danger struts into our yard, threatening
  my chickens or me,
See the hair on my hen's neck get straighter
Just see how much beadier my eyes can get
when I look danger slap in the beak.
Yes I'm a hen
Of course I'm a hen
I don't mind being a hen
I'll tell you one thing I do mind though
– these people coming in here to our yard calling
  me a bird.

One day – funny thing – last week
I met Bessie.
She has no chickens
And I've more chickens than I can count.
We both dropped eggs and it *was* a funny
  thing –
we both said

suddenly —
— as if we'd discussed it before and we hadn't
'I'm not hatching That.' Full stop.
We walked away. Just walked away and left the
 poor eggs there.
No one noticed.

Yes we're hens
Of course we are hens
More than half of Roosterkind is hens
Proud to be hens
Hard to be hens though sometimes
Just you mind you don't call us birds.
Times are hard enough for hens now.
Myself, I don't like clucking about it too much
I only get depressed
I have enough else to depress me what with
 my chickens and all that.

I KNOW there's all those hens stuck in cages
I KNOW they're only battery hens when
 they've finished with them
I KNOW we should do something
EVERYONE who has read THAT book
 knows we should do something
But I don't really have the time.
I don't want to go on about this
I don't want to go overboard or anything
But I think that's maybe why I deserted the egg

that day.
(On top of everything else
You know – all the chickens I've had have been
    roosters.
I mean it's no laughing matter –
36 bloody roosters.
I'll tell you someone who never wants to hear
    that line again
It's another lovely Cock.)

You laugh – easy for you,
I had to rear the damn things as well.
And they'll probably grow up calling me a you
    know what.
Here I'm away, I'm getting depressed.

I AM a hen.
Of course I'm a hen
Proud to be a hen
Please please don't call me a bird.

EVELYN CONLON

Strangeways

G ranny's canary
  Escaped from its cage
It's up on the roof
In a terrible rage

Hurling abuse
And making demands
That granny fails
To understand

'Lack of privacy'
'Boring old food'
It holds up placards
Painted and rude

It's not coming down
The canary warns
Till gran carries out
Major reforms.

The message has spread
And now for days
Cage-birds have been acting
In very strange ways.

ROGER McGOUGH

What Have We Got in the House?

I think I know what we've got in the house.
When it moves, it makes more mess than
 a mouse.
So, what do you think we've got in the house?

We found egg-shell down
By the washing machine
And four claw-prints
In the margarine.

I think I know what we've got in the house.
When it moves, it makes more mess than a
 mouse,
Or a rat, or a roach, or a louse.
So, what do you think we've got in the house?

The sides of the bath
Are greenish-tinged
And the spare toothbrush
Has had its bristles singed.

I think I know what we've got in the house.
When it moves, it makes more mess than a
 mouse,

Or a rat, or a roach, or a louse,
Or a gerbil, or an oyster, or a grouse.
So what do you think we've got in the house?

We've never had a fire
But I often cough.
Then the smoke alarm
In the hall goes off.

I think I know what we've got in the house.
When it moves, it makes more mess then a
  mouse,
Or a rat, or a roach, or a louse,
Or a gerbil, or an oyster, or a grouse,
Or a duck-billed platypus together with its
  spouse.
So, what do you think we've got in the house?

There are long scratch-marks
Just like from claws
Around the handles
Of all the doors.

I think I know what we've got in the house.
Don't you?

NICK TOCZEK

Unicorn

He slipped into my sleep,
Out of the thicket of my dreams,
Timid, white, his single whorled horn,
So special, so innocent,
Like the maiden he was searching for.
His small damp nose sifted the air,
His bright moist eyes
Searched the scene,
As I held my breath, entranced
By the privilege of his presence.
This must be our secret,
I've not told anyone about this:
It might break the spell.

John Cotton

In a Dark Stone

'About seven thousand years ago
There was a little girl
Who looked in a mirror
And thought herself pretty.'

'I don't believe you. All that time ago
If there was a little girl she'd be wild
Wearing skins, and living in damp woods.'

'But seven thousand years ago
When England was a swamp with no one in it,
Long before the Romans,
In other lands by rivers and in plains
People made necklaces and learnt to write
And wrote down their accounts, and made fine
   pots,
Maps of the stars to sail by, and built cities;
And that is where they found this mirror
Where once the Hittite people roamed and ruled.'

'So you were there, were you, all that time ago
And living far from home, in ancient Turkey?'

'No, but I saw this mirror. Here in England.
It was the smallest thing in a large hall
Of great bronze cauldrons, statues, slabs of stone.

You mustn't think that it was made of glass
Common, like our mirrors.   It was
A little lump of stone, shining; black; deep;
Hard like a thick black diamond, but better:
  obsidian.
It would have fitted in the palm of your hand.
One side was shaped and polished, the back
  rough.

Small though it was I crossed the room to see
  it.
I wanted to look in it, to see if it worked
Really, as a mirror, but I waited.'

'Why did you wait till nobody was round you?
You weren't trying to steal it were you?'
              'No. I was scared.

I waited and came slowly to it sideways.
I put my hand in front. It worked as a mirror.

And then I looked into that polished stone.
I thought the shadow of the shape I looked at
Was looking out at me. My face went into
That dark deep stone and joined the other
  face
The pretty one that used to search her mirror
When she was alive thousands of years ago.

I don't think she'd have come if there'd been
   a crowd.
They were all looking at the gold and brass.'

'I wish I could see it. Would she come for me?'

'I think the mirror's back in Turkey now.'

'I'd travel miles and miles if I could see it.'

'Well, nearer home, there were flint mines in
   Norfolk
And just where the land slopes a bit above some
   trees
On the Suffolk–Norfolk border, there's a track
And once I saw . . . But that's another story.'

JENNY JOSEPH

A Feather from an Angel

Anton's box of treasures held
a silver key and a glassy stone,
a figurine made of polished bone
and a feather from an angel.

The figurine was from Borneo,
the stone was from France or Italy,
the silver key was a mystery
but the feather came from an angel.

We might have believed him if he'd said
the feather fell from a bleached white crow,
but he always replied, 'It's an angel's, I know,
a feather from an angel.'

We might have believed him if he'd said,
'An albatross let the feather fall,'
but he had no doubt, no doubt at all,
his feather came from an angel.

'I thought I'd dreamt him one night,' he'd say.
'But in the morning I knew he'd been there;
he left a feather on my bedside chair,
a feather from an angel.'

And it seems that all my life I've looked
for that sort of belief that nothing could shift,
something simple, yet precious as Anton's gift,
a feather from an angel.

Brian Moses

The Fairy Sea

(Traditional Story)

Have you heard the sea bells
Tinkling on the shore
Have you seen the sea shells
Twinkling on the floor
Have you seen the sea horse
Ride the high sea swells
Watched the waves come rolling
Smelt the sweet sea smells?

Have you seen the sea nymph
Rise up upon the tide
Have you seen the greyhound
Run yapping at her side
Have you heard the seagull
That cries upon the wing
Have you heard the sea cow
Heard its cow bell ring?

Have you felt the sea spray
Fall wet upon your hair
Touched the swirling seaweed
Built castles in the air

Have you heard the sea roar
Come raging on the main
Have you heard the sea breeze
Calling out your name?

Pick up a sea shell
Place to your ear
Close your eyes tightly
Now what do you hear?

Patricia P. Jones

A Bargain

The prince said to the pretty girl
 'I think I'll let you be
My bride, my wife, my helpmate,
If you'll simply agree
To have ten children, mend my socks,
Cook kippers for my tea,
Wash out my dirty underwear,
And never nag at me.'

The pretty girl said to the prince,
'You need a wife. I see.
All right, I'll be your partner,
If you'll simply agree
To bring me back last Monday
From the dry part of the sea,
A pair of blue bananas
And a toffee apple tree.'

RICHARD EDWARDS

Mirrors

An aviary of dresses
alive with silk
roosts on
the rail of your wardrobe.

Each day you disturb
the flock,
shake out a flight
of fabrics.

It's your own rainforest,
mimic plumage
from shops,
your several selves,
crimson macaw, blue-foot
booby, albatross

looping the world.

Isobel Thrilling

From Fairy Tales

there was once a princess who fell in love with a handsome young prince, and together they wandered in the wood. but the prince got lost in pine needles, and the princess searched for him, disconsolate.

she met a toad who said, 'come with me and I'll give you shelter.' so she went with the toad.

later the toad said, 'will you sleep in my bed?' so the princess did, but the toad remained a toad.

the princess continued to live with it because it was kind, because she was fond of it and because she was used to it.

one day, along came a handsome young prince. as the princess went off with him, she said to the toad, 'I did so wish you'd turned into a handsome prince,' and the toad said, 'it's all in the mind, lady.'

Lee Cataldi

A place Without Footprints

I'm searching for a place
Without footprints,
But I'm the youngest child.

Whatever I try,
Wherever I go,
Whatever I choose,
One of them has already
Succeeded,
Been there,
Chosen first.
I'm just a comparison,
Usually unfavourable.
Born to follow,
To repeat the pattern,
The footprints are never mine.

But I'll keep moving,
Hoping the direction is new,
Hoping that one day
A space will appear
Like a fresh snowfall,
Untouched,
Unnoticed by the others,

As I'm searching for a place
Without footprints,
As I'm searching for a place
To plant mine.

Daphne Kitching

Image

Old houses were scaffolding once
and workmen whistling.

T. E. HULME

Suit of Armor

In its human shape
Of moulded steel,
It looks as though
There's someone real

Inside. You knock:
'Hello in there,'
And hear a dull
Echo of air

As though a voice
Were drifting through
The lonely centuries
To you.

BEVERLY MCLOUGHLAND

shell

The sea fills my ear
   With sand and with fear.

You may wash out the sand
But never the sound
Of the ghost of the sea
That is haunting me.

TED HUGHES

ARE WE GOING SEPARATE wAYS?

Happiness

So early it's still almost dark out.
    I'm near the window with coffee,
and the usual early morning stuff
that passes for thought.
When I see the boy and his friend
walking up the road
to deliver the newspaper.
They wear caps and sweaters,
and one boy has a bag over his shoulder.
They are so happy
they aren't saying anything, these boys.
I think if they could, they would take
each other's arm.
It's early in the morning,
and they are doing this thing together.
They come on, slowly.
The sky is taking on light,
though the moon still hangs pale over the water.
Such beauty that for a minute
death and ambition, even love,
doesn't enter into this.
Happiness. It comes on
unexpectedly. And goes beyond, really,
any early morning talk about it.

RAYMOND CARVER

75

One-track Mind

Why does she take unnecessary trips?
　　She lives just opposite a row of shops.
She went to Crewe to buy a bag of chips.
She went to Birmingham to buy lamb chops.

She has no time for aeroplanes or boats.
She cannot get enough of British Rail.
She went to Liverpool for Quaker Oats
Then Halifax to buy the *Daily Mail*.

She went to Chester for a pair of tights.
Every weekend she's up and down some track.
She went to York for twenty Marlboro Lights.
She went to Stalybridge and came straight back.

Once, on her way to Hull for cottage cheese,
She saw him. All he said was *Tickets, please*.

SOPHIE HANNAH

Mir Baku

Mir Baku lives at number 22.
He wears a curled-wool, ship-shaped hat
pulled down over his large, furled ears.
He never takes it off
as far as I can see.
He walks to the corner shop
every morning
hunched into his overcoat
(the one with a rip and loads of pockets).
Then he walks back
with a funny-written newspaper,
   two small tins of catfood,
a loaf of lumpy black bread and four
   onions.
Dad says he came from the Soviet Union.
But where's that, nowadays?
Is he a Kazakh? An Uzbek? A Chechen?
Or is he from Azerbaijan?
I'd like to ask,
but Mum says it'd be rude.
So I just call 'Good Morning,'
and watch the fierce brown crinkles
round his eyes
as he smiles at the cats in his window.

LUCY COATS

middle child

The piggy in the middle
The land between sky and sea
The cheese which fills the sandwich
The odd one out of three
The one who gets the hand-me-downs
And broken bits of junk
The follower, not the leader
The one in the bottom bunk

The one for whom the pressure's off
The one who can run wild
The one who holds the balance of power
The lucky second child.

LINDSAY MACRAE

Dad's Night Voice

Why does my dad snore and snore
so? Sometimes I see it is
to have his roar filling
the house, even when he sleeps.

Smiling sometimes I see
his snore is a croaking frog
with a bad cold, which has
taken over Dad's head.

Sometimes I wonder if he is
trying to start up the crowing
of distant cocks, as a boy said
his granddad's snoring used to do.

Other times, I see it as an old
car Dad's managed to get going
oddly, that shuts off only when
Mum shoves him, to sleep on his side.

JAMES BERRY

Dad, Don't Dance

Whatever you do, don't dance, Dad
Whatever you do, don't dance
Don't wave your arms
Like a crazy buffoon
Displaying your charms
By the light of the moon
Trying to romance
A lady baboon
Whatever you do, don't dance

When you try to dance
Your left leg retreats
And your right leg starts to advance
Whatever you do, don't dance, Dad.
Has a ferret crawled into your pants?
Or maybe a hill full of ants?
Don't samba
Don't rumba
You'll tumble
And stumble
Whatever you do, Dad, don't dance

Don't glide up the aisle with a trolley
Or twirl the girl on the till
You've been banned from dancing in Tesco's
'Cos your tango made everyone ill

Whatever you do, don't dance, Dad
Whatever you do, don't dance
Don't make that weird face
Like you ate a sour plum
Don't waggle your hips
And stick out your bum
But most of all – PLEASE –
Don't smooch with Mum!
Whatever the circumstance
Whatever you do –
Dad, don't dance

ROGER STEVENS

Divorce: A Spell to Prevent It

If I avoid the lines and cracks
Between the paving stones;
If I leap from the small dark island
Left by a recent shower
To the safe shore of its neighbouring continent
                    Then it won't happen.

If I leave nothing on my plate;
If I find each lost toy
And every stray piece of paper;
If I behave with no more emotion
Than the clothes I wear;
If, like them, I lurk in cupboards,
Silent and out of the way —
                    Then it won't happen.

If *I* say I'm sorry;
If *I* take the blame;
If I tell them it's *my* fault;
If I pray and pray
And give up chocolate,
                    Then it won't happen.

If I could just invent a joke
Which will make them both laugh
                    Perhaps it won't happen.

If I ignore it
                    it won't happen
If I try harder
                    it won't happen
If I am perfect
                    it won't happen.

LINDSAY MACRAE

Granny

Outside your window
a tall tree grows.
Little string bags of nuts
are swinging from
its lowest branch
you can hear the leaves
shuffling in the grass.

Once you used
to hand nuts
from another tree,
in another garden
and watch the birds feeding.

You were a great magician,
who could make toys
and sweets fall
out of the air to my bed
when a winter was a
great, white place
that lasted and lasted.

Now you sit
smiling at me
in your quiet, skin-shabby
eighty years.

Maybe I am older
Than you just remembered.

Once you taught me
how to shell peas,
sitting with your apron
over your large lap.

And when you went away
I cried
though death
was only a whisper in my mind.

PAM ZINNEMANN-HOPE

Kelly Jane Alone

In faded jeans
and anorak
I walk along
the railway track.

Disused for more than
twenty years,
it calms my thunder-
storm of tears.

The rails are going
who knows where
and I'd go too
but I don't dare.

The voices raised
in disarray
are long ago
and far away.

Wild flowers wave
like tiny flags
and there's a thrush
that drags and drags

a worm from deep
inside the grass.
The clouds are calm
and small, and cross

the sky beyond
a pylon there . . .
and I'd go too
but I don't dare.

The argument
that drove me from
the living room
dies and is gone.

In faded jeans
and anorak
I walk along
the railway track.

FRED SEDGWICK

On the Elevator Going Down

A Caucasian gets on at
        the 17th floor.
He is old, fat and expensively
        dressed

I say hello / I'm friendly.
        He says, 'Hi'.

Then he looks very carefully at
        my clothes.

I'm not very expensively dressed.
I think his left shoe costs more
than everything I am wearing.

He doesn't want to talk to me
        any more.

I think that he is not totally aware
that we are really going down
and there are no clothes after you have
been dead for a few thousand years.

He thinks as we silently travel
down and get off at the bottom
        floor
that we are going separate
        ways.

RICHARD BRAUTIGAN

Answer Phone

Please leave your name.
 I shall call you back.
There is no one here.
Do you have a number?

Do you have a cat?
I have four children.
They keep me busy.
They should be back.

I shall call your number.
My mind is empty.
There is no one there.
Please leave my name.

Please leave my cat.
He has no number.
Do you want four children?
They have names.

Please name your children.
My cat is Rover.
He will call you back.
I keep him busy.

JOHN MOLE

NOW I'M TOO COMPLICATED

Love Without Hope

Love without hope, as when the young bird-catcher
Swept off his tall hat to the Squire's own daughter,
So let the imprisoned larks escape and fly
Singing about her head, as she rode by.

ROBERT GRAVES

Leonardo

Leonardo, painter, taking
  Morning air
    On Market Street
Saw the wild birds in their cages
  Silent in
    The dust, the heat.

Took his purse from out his pocket
  Never questioning
    The fee,
Bore the cages to the green shade
  Of a hill-top
    Cypress tree.

'What you lost,' said Leonardo,
  'I now give to you
    Again,
Free as noon and night and morning,
  As the sunshine,
    As the rain.'

And he took them from their prisons,
  Held them to
    The air, the sky;

Pointed them to the bright heaven.
  'Fly!' said Leonardo.
    'Fly!'

CHARLES CAUSLEY

Fearless Bushmen

The bushmen of the Kalahari desert
Painted themselves on rocks
With wildebeests and giraffes
Thousands of years ago.
And still today they say
To boast is sinful
Arrogance is evil.
And although some say today that they
Are the earliest hunter-gatherers known
They never hunt for sport
They think that's rude,
They hunt for food.

They earn respect by sharing
Being true to their word
And caring.
They refuse to own land but
They can build a house in two days
And take it down in four hours.

Three generations will live together.
A girl will grow up to feed her mother
Who feeds the mother
That once fed her.
To get that food a girl will walk

Upon the hot desert sands
An average of a thousand miles a year.

Their footprints are uniquely small
For people who travel so much
To find melons or mongongo trees,
And those small dark and nimble feet
May spend two days chasing a deer.
Charity, respect and tolerance
Are watchwords for these ancient folk
Who spend their evenings singing songs
Around their campfires.

These hunter–gatherers are fearless
But peaceful,
They will never argue with a mamba snake,
When one is seen heading towards the village
They kiss the Earth
And move the village.

BENJAMIN ZEPHANIAH

Kaleidoscope

It is said that the Great Emperor of
all Emperors
called for his wisest and cleverest people
and told them to go away for ten years
to invent useful things.

Whoever could invent the most useful thing of
all
would win 3500 chocolate biscuits.

Ten years later
there was a queue outside the palace
of the Great Emperor of all Emperors.

One by one,
people were asked in
to show their invention
to the Great Emperor of all Emperors.

One woman had invented
windscreen wipers for spectacles.
'Excellent,' said the Great Emperor,
'very useful for when it's raining,
but not a prize-winner, I'm afraid.'

One man had invented
square tomatoes.
'Very good,' said the Great Emperor
'very useful for putting tomatoes in boxes,
but not a prize-winner, I'm afraid.'

One woman had invented
a pencil that sharpened itself.
'I like it,' said the Great Emperor
'Very useful when you're too tired to use a pencil
  sharpener,
but not a prize-winner, I'm afraid.'

And one man had invented
the kaleidoscope.
'What's this?' said the Great Emperor.
'You look through it,' said the man.
'It's a telescope, is it? Well, I'm afraid
telescopes have already been invented.
Hard luck. Goodbye. Next!'

'It's not a telescope,' said the man,
'but you *do* look through it.'
'What's the point of looking through
something that *looks* like a telescope,
but *isn't* a telescope?' said the Great Emperor.

'You look through it,
then you twist it and move it

and before you know what's what
you find yourself saying, "Ooh!"
Or, on another day,
you might look through it,
twist it and move it
and you could find yourself saying, "Ahhh!"
And I have to tell you this:
sometimes people find themselves saying both
   "Ooh!" *and* "Ahhh!"
'But what's the use of that?' said the Great
   Emperor
'I asked for inventions that are *useful*
not some stupid little thing that makes
you make funny noises.
Thank you and goodbye. Next!'

'Just try it,' said the man.

'Oh, if I must!' said the Great Emperor crossly.
And he picked up the kaleidoscope.
He twisted it and moved it
and he looked through it.
And when he saw all the colours of the rainbow
glowing in there
and when he saw all those patterns
changing over and over again
he said,
'Ooh!'
And then he said,

'Ahhh!'

Then,
as he went on looking through it
and changing the patterns, he said,
'Yes, it's very nice,
but what's it *for*?
Is it *useful*?'

And the man who had invented the kaleidoscope said,
'If you think about it,
it's *very* useful.
People go all over the world to look for things
like the Grand Canyon
or the Eiffel Tower
so that when they see them they will say,
"Ooh!" and "Ahhh!"
With this invention
you won't have to move out of your chair.
All you have to do is carry it in your pocket.
And whenever you feel like a quick "Ooh!"
or a quick "Ahhh!"
you take it out,
look through it
twist it about a bit
and there you are . . .'

But the Great Emperor wasn't listening.
He was too busy

looking through the world's first kaleidoscope
and saying, 'Ooh!' and 'Ahhh!'

Later
much later
the man won 3500 chocolate biscuits.

Well,
that's how the story goes.
It may or may not be true.

MICHAEL ROSEN

Just for Fun

It started with a cactus
From a boot sale, just for fun,
But the cactus looked so lonely
That she bought another one,
Then another, then a cheese plant,
Then some fuchsias, then a fern,
Till Belinda's rooms were bursting –
There was hardly room to turn.

Aspidistras, palms, geraniums, lilies –
More and more and more,
Jasmine creeping through the bathroom,
Ivy trailing on the floor,
'Oooh, how lovely!' said the neighbours,
'It's the prettiest house we've seen.'
'Take some cuttings,' said Belinda,
'We can turn the whole street green.'

Soon each house was like a garden,
Tendrils twined themselves in knots,
Climbed the stairs, explored the attics,
Burst like smoke from chimney pots,
Roots went rootling through the cellars,
Shoots went shooting everywhere,
Huge leaves shouldered up the roof tiles
And escaped into the air.

Down the high street, past the station,
Moved the jungle like a tide,
Chasing shoppers out of Tesco's,
Shoving cars and trucks aside,
Swamping parks, devouring statues,
Rolling on and on and on,
Till the last grey wall was swallowed
And the last grey roof was gone.

First arrivals were some fruit bats,
Then a parakeet flew down
And the howls of monkeys echoed
Round what once had been a town.
Tigers prowl the crumbling ruins,
Tree snakes slither in the sun . . .
And all because Belinda
Bought a cactus, just for fun.

RICHARD EDWARDS

Growing Apples

And the King said,
'How do I turn this apple
into thousands of apples?'

The wise men scratched their heads,
muttered amongst themselves
and consulted their great books.

One stepped forward.
'Perhaps this is some kind of joke,
your majesty,
but could one say
that one could make
a thousand apples
by chopping one apple into a thousand pieces?'

'Balderdash!' said the King
'I said thousands of apples
not some nonsensical business
about hacking an apple to bits.'

Another wise man stepped forward.
'I have heard that beyond the horizon
there lives a man
who sings to the objects in his house
it is said of him

that he can cause things to multiply.
Maybe –'

'Poppycock!' roared the King,
'I wasn't looking for some holy-moly jiggery-
    pokery.'

And on it went.

None of the wise men
were wise enough to solve the problem.

A serving-girl
who was pouring the wine
caught the drift of what was going on.

'I know how to turn your apple
into thousands of apples,' she said.

How the wise men laughed!
'The cheek!'
'A little whipper-snapper like her!'
'As if she'd know!'

'Come then,' said the King,
'Speak, girl!'

'I would bury your apple,'
Said the girl.

There was silence.

The wise men looked at each other
and sniggered.
'Bury it? Bury it?
What good would that do?'

But the King didn't wait.
'You're right, young lady.
Completely and utterly right.'

MICHAEL ROSEN

The Tunneller

At number 42
there's a hawthorn perimeter hedge
and the front gate is topped
with strands of barbed wire.
The mad Major lives there,
a septuagenarian ex-soldier
with military moustache
and a broom-handle straight back.

On a mission,
in the last war, he parachuted into Germany,
was captured, and then held
in a prison camp: Stalag number 39.
He tunnelled out, escaped to England.
His true story is printed in a book
I found at the library:
Spies of the Second World War.

Yesterday,
at dusk, I hid in his long back garden
and spied on the Major
as he passed the old air-raid shelter
and marched into his garden shed.
He was dressed in black –
trousers, sweater, and woolly Balaclava.
Dirt streaks disguised his face.

I sneaked up
and through the cobwebby window
watched as the Major removed floorboards,
then lowered himself into a hole
And . . . disappeared!
He was tunnelling again,
digging beneath his back garden,
tunnelling towards the perimeter hedge.

An hour later
he emerged furtively from the shed
lugging a heavy sack
and I saw him scatter damp soil
between his rhubarb and cauliflowers.
Night after night he's at it,
secretly tunnelling his way to freedom,
trying to escape from Stalag number 42.

WES MAGEE

Dead End

My job? Well, I write
street names. No, not
the actual metal plates.
I make up the names.
Yes, it's interesting
and trickier than you'd think.
To start with, no one wants
them funny, or hard to say,
or spell. You know, the
embarrassment in shops.
And they end in such
limited ways: street, road.
No, I've not had one used yet.
It takes time to make your name.

MICHAEL HARRISON

I Was Afraid to Begin

I was afraid to begin
— pen in hand, notebook open
desk lamp on, rain outside.

There were noises downstairs.
I went to check.
Tyre screeches pierced my window pane.
I looked out.
I went to pee. I went to see. I went to be
doing something else.

What was it feared?
Ignorance, or jest;
words upon this window pane;
discovery, or nothingness?
I was afraid to begin
so I made it a first line.

SEAMUS CASHMAN

A Sort of Chinese Poem

The Chinese write poems
  That don't look like poems.
They are more like paintings.

A cherry-tree, a snow-storm,
An old man in a boat –
These might be their subjects.

It all looks so easy –
But it isn't.
You have to be very simple,
Very straightforward,
To see so clearly.
Also, you have to have thousands of years of skill.

When I was a child, I once wrote a Chinese
  poem.
Now I'm too complicated.

ELIZABETH JENNINGS

Spellbound

I have a spell in chequer
It came with my pea see.
It plane Leigh Marx four my revue
Miss takes eye ken knot sea.
I've run this poem threw IT
I'm shore your plea zed too no;
Its let a perfect in it's weigh
My check her tolled me sew.

NORMAN VANDAL

Shop chat

My shop stocks:
> locks, chips,
> chopsticks,
> watch straps,
> traps, tops,
> taps, tricks,
> ships' clocks,
> lipstick and chimney pots.

What does your shop stock?

Sharkskin socks.

LIBBY HOUSTON

Against Broccoli

The local groceries are all out of broccoli,
Loccoli.

ROY BLOUNT, JR

Lizzie's Road

L ittle Lizzie drew a long, long road
  That curled across the paper like a strange,
  exotic snake.
She decorated it in darkest reds and brightest
  blues,
Gleaming golds and glittering greens.
Mum asked, 'Why all these wonderful colours?'
'These are the rubies and emeralds and pearls,'
  Lizzie explained.
'The diamonds and opals and precious stones.'
'What a wonderful road,' said Mum. 'Is is magic?'
'No,' explained the child. 'It's just a jewel
  carriageway.'

GERVASE PHINN

Everything in its Place

The skeleton is hiding in the closet as it
should,
The needle's in the haystack and the trees are
in the wood,
The fly is in the ointment and the froth is on
the beer,
The bee is in the bonnet and the flea is in the
ear.

The meat is in the coconut, the cat is in the
bag,
The dog is in the manger and the goat is on
the crag,
The worm is in the apple and the clam is on
the shore,
The birds are in the bushes and the wolf is at
the door.

ARTHUR GUITERMAN

I'll Bark Against the Dog-Star

I'll bark against the Dog-star,
And crow away the morning;
  I'll chase the moon
  Till it be noon,
And I'll make her leave her horning.

I'll crack the Poles asunder,
  Strange things I will devise on.
I'll beat my brain against Charles's Wain,
  And I'll grasp the round horizon.

I'll search the caves of Slumber,
  And please her in a night-dream;
I'll tumble her into Lawrence's fen,
  And hang myself in a sunbeam.

I'll sail upon a millstone,
  And make the sea-gods wonder,
I'll plunge in the deep, till I wake asleep,
  And I'll tear the rocks in sunder.

ANONYMOUS

Spell to Summon the Owner of the Shoes

Here are your shoes.

I have mended them with strong thread
I have mended them with all my skill
I have mended them with tough leather
I have mended them with fine leather.

These shoes cannot be worn by anyone
Not by my friends who are barefoot
Not by my friends with lovely faces
Not by the deserving.

It's not a question of eyes or shoulders
It's not a question of images
It's not a question of name or promises
These shoes are for your feet and none other.

May you wear them to shreds
May you wear them to tatters
May you wear holes in them
May you wear them till there is nothing left
  of them

May you cross mountains in them
May you cross cities in them
May you cross moors in them
May you cross fields in them

May you wear them in hot weather
May you wear them in wet weather
May you wear them through snow and ice
May you wear them through mud and slush.

May you wear them on grass
May you wear them on concrete
May you wear them on carpeted floors
May you wear them in good company

May you wear them at night
May you wear them to dance in
May you work in them without aching feet
May you be forever without corns and blisters.

Without you these shoes are useless
Without you they are worthless
Without you they are not special
Without you they are emptiness and clutter

Come and get them.

JENI COUZYN

How to Talk to Trees

Use no words. Instead lie down
Upon the grass, beneath
The swaying boughs. Look up.
Keep looking up. Pay attention
To everything you see. Disregard
All thought and the sense
You should be somewhere else doing
Something else: this has its own
Significance. Do not move.
Do not care. Simply be aware
Of trees . . .
Until, at last,
Your mind starts growing, branching out,
Extending upwards gradually
Towards the sky, towards the sun. Feel it sprout
Leaf
On leaf
On leaf . . .
Let it grow
As high as it will go, as wide
As it will reach – then do
No more. Nothing.
Only stay
Right where you are, your mind
Mingling with the quiet air
And the quiet light . . . Now you will find

That, without really trying,
You'll be talking in a language trees
Can understand — not our language
Of words, but their language
Of peace.

GILLIAN FLOYD

Whosland

At dawn one morn
After eight weeks of sailing,
The Europeans landed
On the gold, sandy beach.

After praying
They made their way
Inland,
With their flags in their hands
And an empire on their minds.

Soon they came across a small village,
All the people came out to see them,
The villagers thought they had come with great
  knowledge
And wisdom from afar.
Having never seen Europeans before
This was new and exciting.

When the captain of the ship
Met the elder of the village
He still had a flag in his hand
And an empire on his mind.

'What did you call this land before
we arrived?'
said the captain.

'Ours'
said the village elder,

'Ours.'

Benjamin Zephaniah

child-body starving story

Head misshapen and patchy with hair
  with shocked eyes in a hole with a stare

cheeks collapsed in skin among bones
  with cracked lips having not one moan

ears keeping a nonstop whining sound
  with neck hardly more than a broom-handle
  hold

hunched up shoulders v-shaped
  with twiggy arms claws-fingered

a belly all self pumped-up
  and knees the knotted marbles thinly skin
  wrapped

legs the drumsticks knee-knockers
  with feet not finding a body to carry
  together –

show me off, as this body-exhibit labelled,
'A NOT-ENOUGH-TO-SHARE
LEFT-OUT'

and other times labelled,
'A GOVERNMENT'S NON-CARING
LEFT-OUT.'

JAMES BERRY

The Sun and the Lizard

You think you've seen a good portion
   of the world and, recalling a recent flight
to the Orient when looking into
the vanishing night you saw the sun's sudden

appearance, think you've got the earth's measure,
that it's a quicker revolution than observed
by the stationary eye, when sitting still
in your garden beside the potted geraniums

you see a lizard raise its head on a branch
of the chinaberry tree and inflate its neck
into a translucent pink pouch, and that's
when you become uncertain of your world,

being reminded how each time you left the movie
theatre after the matinée performance it was
a shock to see the sun still up and the world
not yet abandoned to fantasy.

ZULFIKAR GHOSE

First Morning

I was there on that first morning of creation
when heaven and earth occupied one space
and no one had heard of the human race.

I was there on that first morning of creation
when a river rushed from the belly of an egg
and a mountain rose from a golden yolk.

I was there on that first morning of creation
when the waters parted like magic cloth
and the birds shook feathers at the first joke.

JOHN AGARD

Thoughts Like an Ocean

The sea comes to me on the shore
   On lacy slippered feet
And shyly, slyly slides away
With a murmur of defeat.

And as I stand there wondering
Strange thoughts spin round my head
Of why and where and what and when
And if not, why, what then?

Where do lobsters come from?
And where anemones?
And are there other worlds out there
With other mysteries?

Why do *I* walk upon dry land
While fishes haunt the sea?
And as I think about their lives
Do they too think of me?

Why is water, water?
Why does it wet my hand?
Are there really as many stars
As there are grains of sand?

And where would the ocean go to
If there were no gravity?
And where was I before I lived?
And where's eternity?

Perhaps the beach I'm standing on
Perhaps this stretch of sand
Perhaps the Universe itself
Lies on someone else's hand?

And isn't it strange how this water and I
At this moment happened to meet
And how this tide sweeps half the world
Before stopping at my feet.

GARETH OWEN

Steam in the Kettle

Steam in the kettle,
Steam in the pan,
Tell me, tell me
If you can,
As through the white air
You boil and blow –
Where do you come from
And where do you go?

Steam from a tower,
Steam from a train,
You smudge the sky
And are gone again.
Up in the air
You straggle and fly,
But when I call
You never reply.

Steam in the iron
And in the machine,
Keep my clothes
Both neat and clean;
But when your work
Is over and done
As frail as a ghost
You're faded and gone.

Steam from the pipe
And smoke from the stack,
Send me a signal
Of white or black.
You float like a feather
Over the green,
And then it's as if
You never had been.

Mist in the meadow
And fume in the street
– One so bitter
And one so sweet –
What will you write
On the page of day
Before you silently
Hurry away?

Mist and fume
And smoke and steam
– Wilder than water
From sea or stream –
Wandering low
And wandering high
On city stone
Or in country sky:

I see your breath
On the window-pane,

Or crossing the clouds
Like an aeroplane,
Sometimes near
And sometimes far –
Tell me, tell me
Who you are!

Fume and mist
And steam and smoke –
You never heard
A word I spoke;
But till the seven seas
Stop their flow
And the wheeling world
Is turned to snow,
I'll ask you what
I want to know:
Where do you come from
And where do you go?

CHARLES CAUSLEY

On Visiting a Natural History Museum

Will superior beings preserve us in glass,
spread the pretty colours of our hair,
while at our sides those televisions pass

for pets? Will we be laid out in the mass,
shown to the young who've acquired a
    questionnaire,
will superior beings preserve us in glass?

Will we be naked or clothed between rails of
    brass,
in graded shades like butterflies in the glare,
while at our sides those televisions pass

for companions? Outside offspring will sit on
    grass,
discuss how well we're stuffed, each specimen
    rare.
Will superior beings preserve us? In glass

our pigments could be stunning, if everyone has
eyelids propped open, irises ranged in a stare,
while at our sides those televisions pass

for keepers. Admired by creatures from space, alas,
we were unwary, proclaimed our planet was there.
Will superior beings preserve us in glass,
while aged aliens enter free with a pass?

ISOBEL THRILLING

ACKNOWLEDGEMENTS

The editor and publishers gratefully acknowledge permission to reproduce copyright material in this book. Every effort has been made to trace and contact copyright holders, but in a few cases this has proved impossible. The editor and publishers apologise for these unwilling cases of copyright transgression and would like to hear from any copyright holders not acknowledged.

'Listen Mr Oxford Don' by John Agard from *Mangoes and Bullets*, published by Serpent's Tail 1990, by kind permission of John Agard c/o Caroline Sheldon Literary Agency, copyright © John Agard 1990; 'First Morning' by John Agard from *Another Day on Your Fott and Would've Died*, published by Macmillan Children's Books, by kind permission of John Agard c/o Caroline Sheldon Literary Agency, copyright © John Agard 1997; 'Poem for the Changing of the Clocks' by Gerard Benson from *To Catch an Elephant*, published by Smith-Doorstop 2002, by permission of the author, copyright © Gerard Benson 2002; 'Against Broccoli' by Roy Blount Jr. published in and by *The Atlantic Monthly*, reprinted by permission of International Creative Management, Inc., copyright ©

INDEX OF FIRST LINES

'About seven thousand years ago   58

A Caucasian gets on at   88

An aviary of dresses   66

And the King said   105

A noise in the house   11

Anton's box of treasures held   6

At dawn one morn   123

At four in the morning   50

At number 42   108

'Come,' said the King   9

'Far away is where I've come from,'
    said the wind   10

Granny's canary   54

Have you heard the sea bells   63

Head misshapen and patchy
    with hair   125

Here are your shoes   119

He slipped into my sleep   57

His head was a helmet   42

If I avoid the lines and cracks   82

I have a spell in chequer   113

I'll bark against the Dog-star   118

I'm a hen   51

I'm a really rotten reader   23

I'm searching for a place   68

In faded jeans   86

In its human shape   71

I think I know what we've got
  in the house   55

It is said that the Great Emperor
  of all Emperors   98

It started with a cactus   103

I was afraid to begin   111

I was daydreaming   38

I was there on that first
  morning of creation   128

Josie, Josie, I am okay   33

Leonardo, painter, taking   94

Little Lizzie drew a long,
  long road   116

Love without hope, as when
  the young bird-catcher   93

Me not no Oxford don   27

Mir Baku lives at number 22   77

My father left us in the dead
  of winter   6

My job? Well, I write   110

My shop stocks   114

Old houses were scaffolding once   70

Outside your window   84

Paula is tidy   35

People said, 'Indian children are
  hard to teach'   29

Piggy to Joey   39

Please leave your name   90

She'd always had a baggy skin   48
So early it's still almost dark out   75
Steam in the kettle   131
The bushmen of the Kalahari desert 96
The cat lies low, too scared   16
The Chinese write poems   112
The dark is only a blanket   12
The good thing about friends   36
The local groceries are all out
    of broccoli   115
The mothers are waiting in the
    yard   18
The piggy in the middle   78
The prince said to the pretty girl   65
There was a boy at school we
    called 'Lucky'   45
there was once a princess who
    fell in   67
The sea comes to me on the
    shore   129
The sea fills my ear   72
The skeleton is hiding in the
    closet as it should   117
This hour   13
'This morning,' cries Miss Creedle   19
Use no words. Instead lie down   121
Whatever you do, don't dance,
    Dad   80

What happens when the gates
  are locked   17
'What's that creature that rattles
  the roof?'   15
What's your colour, the colour
  of your skin   31
When I'm dancing   8
Why does my dad snore and snore   79
Why does she take unnecessary
  trips?   76
Why is just a minute   3
Will superior beings preserve us
  in glass   134
Word is out on the street tonight   43
You know how sometimes   5
'You look good in glasses.'   7
You're late. Take a chance up
  the cul-de-sac   40
You think you've seen a
  good portion   127

INDEX OF POETS

Agard, John   27, 128
Anonymous   118
Bell, Juanita   29
Benson, Gerard   13
Berry, James   33, 79, 125
Blount, Jr, Roy   115
Brautigan, Richard   88
Carver, Raymond   75
Cashman, Seamus   111
Cataldi, Lee   67
Causley, Charles   94, 131
Clarke, Gillian   16
Coats, Lucy   77
Conlon, Evelyn   51
Cotton, John   57
Couzyn, Jeni   119
Dixon, Peter   23
Donaldson, Julia   31
Duffy, Carol Ann   12
Durant, Alan   7, 48
Edwards, Richard   65, 103
Floyd, Gillian   121
Ghose, Zulfikar   127
Graves, Robert   93
Greygoose, David   15
Gross, Philip   40
Guiterman, Arthur   117
Hannah, Sophie   76
Harrison, Michael   110

Hoban, Russell 10
Houston, Libby 114
Hughes, Ted 72
Hulme, T. E. 70
Jennings, Elizabeth 112
Jones, Brian 36
Jones, Patricia P. 63
Joseph, Jenny 58
Jubb, Mike 38
Kitching, Daphne 68
Knight, Stephen 6, 11, 17
MacRae, Lindsay 3, 35, 78, 82
Magee, Wes 108
McGough, Roger 45, 54
McLoughland, Beverly 71
McMillan, Ian 5
Middleton, Christopher 18
Mitchell, Adrian 42, 50
Mole, John 90
Moses, Brian 43, 61
Owen, Gareth 19, 129
Phinn, Gervase 116
Rice, John 9
Rosen, Michael 98, 105
Sedgwick, Fred 8, 86
Smith, Stevie 39
Stevens, Roger 80
Thrilling, Isobel 66, 134
Toczek, Nick 55
Vandal, Norman 113
Zephaniah, Benjamin 96, 123
Zinnemann-Hope, Pam 84